BBC toybox

Bumper Story Book 2

BBC CHILDREN'S BOOKS

ISBN 0 563 38057 8

First published 1997

This presentation copyright © BBC Children's Books 1997

Contents

Pingu Goes to Playgroup

Pinga was cross. Everyone had forgotten that it was her first day at playgroup today.

"Hurry up!" she cried, as she stood ready by the door. "I want to go."

"Oh, my goodness," said Mum. "I'd forgotten all about it. Pingu had better take you."

"Pingu!" yelled Pinga. "I want you to take me to playgroup NOW!"

"All right, all right," said Pingu. "Let's go."

Playgroup had already started by the time Pingu and Pinga arrived.

"I'm sorry we're late," squeaked Pinga.

"That's all right, little Pinga," smiled the teacher. "Don't worry."

"You must be Pinga's brother," she said to Pingu. "Perhaps you'd like to stay for a while and join in the fun this morning."

"Actually, I think I'm a little bit too old for playgroup," said Pingu.

"Please stay, Pingu," said Pinga. "I'm feeling rather scared."

"Well, all right then," said Pingu.

Pingu and Pinga made their way across the classroom to some empty seats. Pinga held her brother's hand tightly.

"Today we are going to make paper hats," said the teacher. "Just copy me."

"Come on, Pinga," said Pingu. "That looks fun."

Pinga looked at her brother in panic. "I can't do it," she said in a worried voice.

"Don't worry, I'll help you," said Pingu.

He went up to the teacher to ask for some paper of his own. He folded the paper quickly, making a hat for Pinga and then one of his own. He was beginning to enjoy himself!

The little penguins were all very pleased with their hats.

"Look at me!" they shouted to each other.

"Now we're going to do some dancing," said the teacher. She put a record on and the little penguins all clapped their hands and marched along in time to the music. Pingu joined in too and had a wonderful time.

After the dancing, it was playtime. Pingu had a go on the slide first. He zoomed down it head first and went shooting off the end.

"Ha, ha!" laughed Pinga who was sitting at the top of the slide with a new friend.

Everybody felt rather tired after all that running around, so they were very pleased when the teacher announced that it was story time.

"Sit down, everyone, and make yourselves comfortable," said the teacher. She pulled up a chair and opened a big book.

The little penguins sat quietly in a row while the teacher read them an exciting tale all about a snowman. Pingu enjoyed it just as much as everyone else.

"That was great," he said.

At last it was time to go home.

"You've all been very good this morning," said the teacher as she waved her class goodbye. "See you tomorrow."

"Goodbye, Pinga," said the teacher. "I hope you enjoyed having your brother at playgroup this morning."

"Oh, yes," said Pinga, "but he's a bit too big for it really."

"Thank you," said Pingu to the teacher as he left. "Playgroup is a lot of fun. You know, I wish I wasn't too big for it!"

William and the Friendly Ghost

One night, William's bedtime story was about ghosts.
"I'd like to see a real ghost," he thought to himself.
"It wouldn't scare me!"
William pulled on his wellingtons and made a wish.

Straight away, he found himself in a mysterious, creepy old house. It looked very haunted.

"Too-woo!" called an owl. "Follow me if you want to see a ghost!"

Suddenly, William heard a loud cry. "Woooh!"

"Oh, look!" he cried. "It's the ghost! Come on, owl, let's catch him!"

The ghost didn't want to be caught. It flew up to the
ceiling and disappeared into the loft. William wished for
a hole in the ceiling and some stairs. Then he ran up to
the loft. The ghost flew round and round in a panic,
looking for somewhere to hide.

"Why is he doing that?" asked William.

"He's scared of you," said the owl, as the ghost hid in
an old chest.

"I don't want to scare anyone," said William. "I'll wish for a train set so I can play with him."

"What a nice idea," said the ghost, popping out of the train's funnel. "This must be a ghost train!"

William laughed. "Why were you scared of me?"

"Your boots frightened me," said the ghost.

William laughed. "I'm supposed to be frightened of *you*, ghost – except you aren't scary at all."

"I can't be a very good ghost if you're not scared of me," said the ghost, sadly.

"You're just different," said William. "I like you. Let's be friends."

The ghost was very happy. It liked having a friend.

"Too-woo!" hooted the owl.

Back at home, William heard a noise outside his bedroom. It was his mum.

"Can't you sleep, William?" she asked. "Ghosts aren't real. Don't be scared."

William smiled as she went out of the room.

"I'm not scared – thanks to my wish wellingtons!"

Oakie Doke and the Treasure Hunt

One morning Oakie Doke had a visit from Snoot, Root and Hickory. They all looked very miserable.

"What's happened?" asked Oakie.

"Nothing," replied Hickory. "That's just the point."

"We're bored," explained Snoot.

"There's nothing to do," said Root.

"I see," said Oakie. "Well, in that case, I think we should have a treasure hunt."

"What's that?" asked Hickory.

"It's a game you can play with your friends," said Oakie. "Ask them all to come here and I'll tell you what to do."

In no time at all, Snoot, Root and Hickory had gathered all their friends in Oakie Hollows to hear about the treasure hunt.

"Right," said Oakie. "Now each team has to collect four things – an oak leaf, a feather, a pine cone and a conker. When you've got them all, run back here. The first team to come back wins a little prize."

"Ooh!" said Root.

"Are you ready?" asked Oakie.

"Yes!" cried everyone.

"Then take your marks, get set, GO!" shouted Oakie.

Everyone ran off to start hunting. Snoot, Root and Hickory were in a team together. Before long Hickory found an oak leaf. Then Snoot came across a pine cone and Root spotted a big conker.

"I bet we're going to win!" said Snoot.

"All we need now is a feather," said Hickory.

Snoot and Hickory wandered off to look for a feather, while Root stood still and admired his conker.

"It's the biggest conker I've ever seen," he said, proudly.

Root was just setting off to join the others when he tripped over and let go of his conker. The conker rolled along the ground and fell into a manhole.

"Oh, bother! Bother, bother, bother!" exclaimed Root.

He peered nervously over the edge of the manhole. "It's a long way down," he said. "And it's very dark. But I shall have to go down there to get my conker."

Snoot and Hickory suddenly realised that Root had disappeared. They searched all around, but there was no sign of him anywhere. They ran home to tell their mum and found Oakie Doke there, too.

"Oh, Oakie!" cried Snoot. "Root has gone missing.
One minute he was there carrying a conker and the
next moment . . ."

"There he wasn't," finished Hickory.

"Well," said Oakie, looking at their anxious faces.
"It *was* a treasure hunt, but now I think we had better
organise a Root hunt!"

Oakie Doke sent everyone off in different directions
to look for Root. Oakie himself rode round on his
scooter, shouting out Root's name. Suddenly, Manny
Mole popped out of a manhole right next to him.

"Hello, Manny," said Oakie. "I don't suppose you've seen Root around anywhere?"

"As a matter of fact, I have," said Manny. He pulled Root out of the manhole.

Root explained what had happened with the conker.

"It fell down the hole and I had to rescue it," he said. "It's the biggest conker I've ever seen."

"Well, thank goodness you're safe!" cried Oakie in relief.

Oakie Doke took Root straight home on his scooter.

"Root!" shouted Rose Corncracker, happily, when she saw him.

"We were all really worried about you, Root," said Rose. "We thought you were lost."

"I wasn't really lost, Mum," said Root. "I just took a bit of a wrong turning while we were doing the treasure hunt."

Root held up a silver spoon that he had been carrying in his hand.

"Look!" he cried. "I found some real treasure while I was down Mr Mole's tunnel."

"Well done, Root," said Oakie. "Now that's what I call a *real* treasure hunt!"

Dinobabies and the Flying Lesson

Franklin was tired of being the scaredy Dinobaby. He really wanted his little brother, Marshall, to be proud of him. So he decided to do something very brave. Franklin decided he wanted to learn how to fly. Stanley had given him two big palm leaves for wings, and Marshall had made him a pointy beak out of another leaf.

"Fly now!" chorused the Dinobabies.

Just then, Dak flew up to see what was going on.

"Franklin's going to fly," said Stanley.

"No way," laughed Dak. "He's not smart enough to fly."

"I *am*!" shouted Franklin, jumping into the air. "He-e-eelp!" he cried as he started to fall.

"Shake your wings off and grab hold of my feet," shouted Dak.

But as he shook his wings, Franklin stopped falling. And soon, he found he was flying.

The other Dinobabies were thrilled that Franklin could fly, but he didn't want to play with them. He wanted to play flying games with Dak.

"You don't have to play with them now you can fly," said Dak. "Come with me and grab some gooey, squashy melons. You'll soon find out that flying games are much more fun."

Franklin grabbed a melon in each hand and flew after Dak. They flew over the other Dinobabies and dropped the gooey melons on their heads! Then they flew away, laughing.

"I'm not going to forget this," said LaBrea, angrily.

But Dak and Franklin were already off playing another game – with a T-Rex!

"My mum said I wasn't to play this game, but *you* could play it," said Dak. "It's the best game of all. Wrap this vine round and round the T-Rex. It will take ages for it to break free. Then you fly off and watch it get cross and roar."

"That sounds like fun," said Franklin. He flew over to the T-Rex and wound the vine round its arms and head.

"Ha, ha!" he laughed, as the T-Rex roared.

But just then, one of Franklin's leaf wings broke in two and he fell into a bush.

"Help! Help me!" cried Franklin, as the T-Rex broke free of the vine. "Dak, help me! I'm stuck in this bush!"

"Erm, I've got to go now," said Dak. "See you later."

"Help! Help!" screamed Franklin, as the T-Rex drew closer.

Just in time, Truman and Stanley heard his cries and they came and pulled him out of the bush.

"RUN!" shouted Truman, as the angry T-Rex crushed the bushes beneath its feet.

The three Dinobabies fled as fast as their feet would carry them.

When they were out of danger, Franklin started to feel ashamed.

"Thank you for helping me and still being my friends, even though I played a trick on you," he said. "I'm never going to fly again, not after that. It was really scary. But now I know who my friends are."

"Well," said Truman, "I'm afraid there's something really scary waiting for you at the treecave."

"What's that?" said Franklin, in a worried voice.

"ME!" shouted LaBrea. She hadn't forgotten about the gooey, squashy melon!

Noddy and the Giraffes

It was a cold day in Toyland, and Noddy was very pleased he was wearing his warm, woolly scarf.

"Hello, Mrs Noah," he called, as he arrived at the Noah's Ark. "I've brought two long scarves from Dinah Doll for the giraffes."

"Giraffes don't wear scarves," said the giraffes, snootily. "We would look silly."

"You must wear scarves whether you like it or not," said Mrs Noah. "I don't want you to get sore throats."

"If anyone tries to make us wear scarves," said the giraffes, "we shall dig in our hooves!"

The next morning, Noddy went to pick up some rope from Sammy Sailor.

"Look," said Sammy. "Someone climbed up the masts and nibbled the flags during the night."

"That's funny," said Noddy. "Someone knocked a brick off the roof of my house last night. I wonder if it was the same very tall someone?"

"Och, no, Noddy!" chortled Sammy. "No one's that tall!"

But when Noddy took the rope to Mr Sparks, he found him replacing the sign above his garage. It had been knocked down during the night.

"I think it must have been knocked down by a very tall someone," said Noddy, and he went to find Mr Plod.

"Someone knocked this bush over last night," grumbled Mr Plod.

"Well, that same tall someone knocked a brick off my roof, chewed the flags on the ships and knocked Mr Sparks' sign down," said Noddy.

Just then, Mrs Noah came running up.

"Mr Plod!" she cried. "Our giraffes are missing! They pulled off their new scarves and ran away."

"Giraffes are tall animals," said Noddy, excitedly. "This could be the key to the Toyland mysteries!"

"This is a tricky case," said Mr Plod. "I'll sleep on it."

Later that night, strange things were happening in the Dark Wood. The goblins were eating jam sandwiches when they heard a crashing sound.

"Monsters!" shrieked Sly and Gobbo, and they ran to hide up the tree.

Lord and Lady Giraffe were feeling hungry and they followed the trail of the goblins' jam sandwiches, right into the old oak tree.

"I'm not staying here," whispered Gobbo. "I'm going to tell Mr Plod about those monsters!"

"I'm too scared to move," whimpered Sly.

Next morning, Noddy went to ask Mr Plod if the giraffes had been found.

Just then, Gobbo came rushing up.

"Help! Help! There are monsters in the wood!" he cried. "Great tall monsters with long necks that eat jam sandwiches!"

"Great tall monsters with long necks?" asked Noddy. "They must be the giraffes."

"We must go and rescue them at once," said Mr Plod, and they all set off for the Dark Wood.

Sly was very relieved to see everyone.

"The monsters are in there," he said, shakily.

"Help!" cried the giraffes. "We're lost in this tree!"

Noddy had an idea. He went into the tree with Mr Plod's torch. "Bend down your necks," he said to the two lost giraffes. "Now, follow me."

A few moments later, Noddy walked out of the tree leading Lord and Lady Giraffe with his scarf.

"Monsters!" shrieked the goblins, running away.

"There you are," Noddy said to the giraffes. "Thanks to my scarf, you're free."

"Scarves aren't so bad after all," said Lord and Lady Giraffe. "We will go back to the ark and ask Mrs Noah to give us our own scarves after all."

"Dear me, Noddy," said Mr Plod. "That was a brilliant rescue, but look how those giraffes have stretched your scarf."

"Never mind," said Noddy. "Now I can wrap it round and round, and it will keep me warm all over. I don't look silly, do I?"

Mr Plod started to giggle when he saw what Noddy had done. "No, Noddy – ha, ha, ha! You don't look silly at all – ha, ha, ha!"

Pingu Wants a Holiday

One day Pingu felt like going on holiday. He decided to build an ice-yacht and travel to somewhere warm.

Pingu locked himself into the shed and started to make some adjustments to his sledge. Before long, the ice-yacht was nearly ready. Then he went into the kitchen and took a loaf of bread and a fish to eat on his journey. He put it into the barrel, then went out to find a sheet he could use as a sail.

Pinga had been watching Pingu's actions with great interest. As soon as he went off to find his sail, she shot into the shed. When she saw the ice-yacht, she was very alarmed.

"He's not going anywhere without me!" she said. Pinga took the fish and the loaf of bread out of the barrel and hid them in a nearby crate. Then she jumped into the barrel herself and hid.

At last everything was ready for Pingu's journey, and he decided to set off.

Pingu felt very excited as he travelled along. He could just imagine stepping into the warm sea and lying on the beach in the shade of a palm tree.

But after a while, he began to feel tired. It was hard work pushing the ice-yacht uphill. Pingu couldn't understand why it felt so heavy. He decided to take a break and have a snack at the top of the hill.

"What shall I have first – some bread, or the fish?" wondered Pingu to himself.

But before Pingu could get out his food, Pinga
sprang out of the top of the barrel like a jack-in-
a-box.

"Hello!" she cried, feeling extremely pleased with
herself. "It's me!"

But Pingu wasn't pleased to see her.

"What are you doing here, and where is all my
food?" he shouted.

"I wanted to come with you so there wasn't any
room for the food," said Pinga.

"But what are we going to eat?" said Pingu.

"I've brought two lollipops," said Pinga.

"Well, that's all right then," said Pingu, tucking
in to his lollipop.

Soon Pingu set off again, pushing Pinga on the ice-yacht. After a while, they came to a big signpost. Pingu stared helplessly at it. He didn't know which way to go.

Pinga began to cry. "I'm hungry and cold," she sobbed. "I thought a holiday would be fun."

"Don't worry, little Pinga," said Pingu, trying to comfort her. "I'll take you home now. We can go on holiday some other time."

So Pingu and Pinga set off back home.

It took a long time to get home, but at last Pingu and Pinga could see the warm lights of the igloo ahead of them.

"Hurray!" they cried.

Mum was delighted to see them both.

"I was beginning to wonder where you two had got to," she said, smiling at them. "You're back just in time for tea!"

Soon all three of them were sitting round the table, eating Mum's cake.

"Holidays sound like a good idea," said Pingu, happily. "But I'm sure the food is better at home!"

William and the Camel

William and Barksure were both playing in the sandpit. William was trying to build a sandcastle.

"I need some more space," said William. "I wish I was in the desert."

And William's wish came true! Straight away, William found himself in the desert. First he built an enormous sandcastle. Then he saw a little camel coming towards him. It looked very unhappy.

"I can't find the oasis where I live with my mum and dad," said the camel, bursting into tears.

"Don't worry," said William. "I'll help you find it."

William and the camel set off to find the oasis. They walked and walked under the desert sun.

It was hot work looking for the oasis and William decided that they needed an ice-cream to keep cool.

He made a wish and an ice-cream seller appeared.

"Two raspberry lollies, please," cried William. "Then we'd better get going again."

William and the camel trekked for miles across the sand.
They began to feel very tired.

"I know," said William. "I'll wish for a ship to take us to
the oasis!"

And all at once William and the little camel were sailing
along in a smart land-yacht.

At last the oasis was in sight.

"That's my home," said the little camel, happily. She rushed up to her mum and dad who were very pleased to see her safely back again.

"Thank you, William," they said.

"That's all right," said William. "I rather enjoyed having a desert adventure with my wish wellingtons."

At last it was time for William to go home. He made a wish and waved goodbye.

"That itchy sand gets everywhere," he complained, as he poured it out of his boots.

"And there's nothing you can do about it – even if you have a pair of magic wish wellingtons!"

Oakie Doke and the Birthday Cake

Early one morning in Oakie Hollows, Lizzie Tickle was paying a visit to Oakie Doke.

"Can you help me, Oakie?" she asked. "Mum is poorly and she needs some of Grannie Annie's special cold and flu medicine."

"I'll go and get the medicine for you," said Oakie at once. "Then you can go home and look after your mum and Libby and Shrimp."

"Thank you, Oakie," said Lizzie.

Oakie went straight off to see Grannie Annie, who was having breakfast with Abel.

"Oakie Doke!" cried Grannie Annie. "What brings you round these parts so early in the morning?"

"Mrs Tickle needs some of your cold and flu medicine," explained Oakie. "She's not very well."

"Poor Mrs Tickle," said Grannie Annie. "And poor Lizzie. It's her birthday today and now there's no one to make her a birthday cake."

"Oh, yes there is!" said Oakie. "I'll go and ask Rose Corncracker if she'll make a cake. She's a great cook."

Oakie Doke went to see if Rose Corncracker was at home.

"She's not here, Mr Doke," squeaked Root.

"Oh, dear," said Oakie, sadly. "I was going to ask her if she could bake a cake for Lizzie Tickle. It's her birthday today and her mum's poorly."

"We can still make a cake," said Albert. "Even if Rose isn't here."

"What a good idea," said Oakie.

"I'll go and get Mum's cookery book," said Hickory. "That will tell us how to do it."

"We will make Lizzie the best birthday cake in the world!" cried Root.

Oakie Doke looked at the recipe and began to make the cake. Root tipped in the flour first which made Oakie sneeze and sneeze.

"Bless you!" cried Snoot.

Soon all the ingredients were in the bowl and Oakie Doke began to beat the mixture furiously.

"That's what I call mixing," said Hickory.

"'Bake for thirty minutes in a hot oven'," Oakie read out from the recipe book. "That will just give us time to get ourselves smartened up for Lizzie's party!"

As soon as the cake was ready, Oakie Doke and the Corncrackers rushed round to Lizzie Tickle's house with the birthday cake.

"Happy birthday, Lizzie!" they all cried out.

"Hello, everyone. What are you doing here?" Lizzie asked.

Lizzie looked very pleased to see them. Then she noticed what Root was carrying.

"What's that?" she asked.

"It's a birthday cake," said Root, proudly. "We made it specially for you. And I got to lick the bowl!"

But as Root walked towards Lizzie, he tripped over and fell head first into the cake!

"Root!" cried everyone.

Root licked his lips and swallowed some of the cake. "It still tastes really yummy," he said as he looked up.

"Oh, dear," said Oakie.

Lizzie was very upset to see her special birthday cake ruined.

"Thank you anyway," she said, bravely. "It was really kind of you."

Suddenly, Mrs Tickle came out of the house with Grannie Annie.

"Mum!" cried Lizzie. "Shouldn't you be in bed?"

"I've had some of Grannie Annie's medicine," said Mrs Tickle. "I feel a lot better."

Then Mrs Tickle caught sight of the squashed birthday cake. Lizzie explained what had happened.

"You didn't think I would forget my Lizzie's birthday, did you?" said Mrs Tickle.

At that very moment, Libby came out carrying a beautiful birthday cake for Lizzie. Mrs Tickle had made it the day before.

"Happy birthday, Lizzie!" cried everyone. "Happy birthday!"

Dinobabies and the Island

The Dinobabies were feeling a little bored when Dak flew up with exciting news.

"I've discovered a secret island," he cried. "Come and explore it."

"It sounds like fun, but we can't swim," said the Dinobabies. "How would we get there?"

Dak dropped a long vine on the ground. "Everyone grab hold of the vine and I'll fly you all there," he said, and they set off.

The Dinobabies gasped when they saw the island.

"It's beautiful," said LaBrea.

"Let's look around," said Truman. "I bet there are some great games we could play."

Suddenly, Stanley noticed Dak flying off.

"Dak! Come back!" he cried. But Dak just laughed.

"How will we get home now?" said Franklin, starting to panic.

"Calm down," said LaBrea. "We'll find a way."

"I know," said Truman. "Let's have a raft-building competition! We can float home on the winning raft."

"May the best raft win!" chorused the Dinobabies, and off they went.

Marshall and Franklin decided to make a raft from lily pads.

"If they float for frogs, they'll float for us," reasoned Franklin.

Truman and LaBrea decided to build a strong, safe raft from rocks.

Meanwhile, Stanley saw a beaversaurus building a dam out of sticks.

"That beaversaurus knows what it's doing," he thought. "I'll copy it and build my raft out of wood."

Before long, it was time to judge the competition. Marshall and Franklin were sure they'd win, and they put their raft of lily pads on the water. But when they jumped on it, it sank underneath them!

Truman and LaBrea heaved their raft into the water. It sank without a trace.

"Ooops," said LaBrea.

Then the Dinobabies inspected Stanley's wooden raft.

"It's got holes in it," said Franklin, worriedly.

"That doesn't matter," said Stanley.

He dropped the raft into the water and jumped on it. Stanley's raft floated!

"Hurray!" cried the Dinobabies. "Let's go home!"

Soon the Dinobabies were paddling home on the wooden raft. Suddenly, Marshall gave a cry.

"Look! There's a monster in the water!"

"A monster!" shrieked the other Dinobabies.

Sure enough, a huge monster popped its head out of the water and looked at the Dinobabies.

"Hi," it said. "Do you want a push home?"

"You're friendly!" said Franklin, in relief. "Yes please, we'd love a push home."

The monster whooshed them across the water.

"My name's Nessie," she said. "Any time you need a lift, just call my name."

The Dinobabies were delighted with their new friend. And they were back on dry land before they knew where they were.

"Thank you," cried the Dinobabies, waving goodbye to Nessie, the friendly monster.

"My pleasure," said Nessie. "I always like to help."

"Well," said Truman, "even though Dak played a naughty trick on us, I rather enjoyed our island adventure. We've had fun after all!"

Noddy Gets a New Job

It was a lovely sunny morning in Toyland, but Mr Plod wasn't feeling very happy. He had fallen off a ladder and bumped his head.

"The doctor has told me to stay in bed for three days. Big-Ears, you will have to look after Toy Town and make sure that everybody behaves," said Mr Plod. "You shall wear my own helmet. Noddy, you can help him too. It is very hard work directing the traffic *and* watching out for thieves."

Noddy and Big-Ears set to work.

"There isn't much traffic to direct today," said Big-Ears.

"In that case, I am going to practise with the pedestrians," said Noddy. "Halt, Martha Monkey. Let Jumbo pass."

"You really are very silly indeed," said Martha. "You haven't even got a helmet."

"Oh," said Noddy, crestfallen.

"Never mind, Noddy," said Big-Ears. "I shall direct the traffic now."

But just then, Mr Sparks drove up.

"Oh, Big-Ears!" cried Mr Sparks. "I have come to report a burglary! Two of my bicycles have been stolen."

"Goodness gracious," said Big-Ears, unhappily. "I don't know what to do. I am so busy directing the traffic."

"Don't worry," said Noddy. "I'm a policeman today too. I shall catch the robbers for you."

"Please be careful!" said Big-Ears.

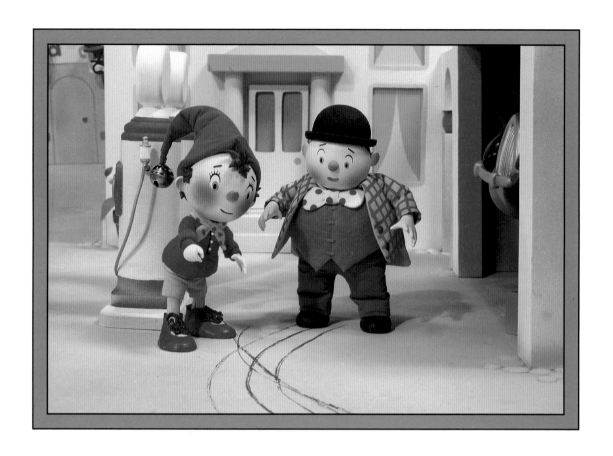

At Mr Sparks' garage, Noddy was making good progress.

"Look," he said. "It was raining last night and there are muddy tyre tracks down here. The robbers must have hopped on the bicycles and ridden away up the road."

"You *are* clever," said Mr Sparks.

"I wonder what I should do now?" pondered Noddy. "I know! I am going to follow these tyre tracks in my little car. They'll lead me to the robbers, and then I can arrest them! Goodbye, Mr Sparks. I'll catch the naughty thieves who stole your bicycles."

Noddy started to follow the muddy tyre tracks down the country road.

"I'm sure that I'm on the right trail," he said to himself.

Eventually, the muddy tracks left the road and went into one of Farmer Straw's fields. Then they stopped suddenly, under an old oak tree.

"This is silly," said Noddy to himself. "Bicycles can't just disappear into the air."

Then Noddy looked up.

"Oh! Perhaps they *can* disappear into the air!" he cried.

The bicycles were hidden up in the branches of the oak tree.

Then Noddy heard a loud snoring sound coming from inside the hollow tree. There were Sly and Gobbo, the goblins, fast asleep!

"I must stop the goblins from escaping until Big-Ears can help me to arrest them," thought Noddy. "I know! I'll trap them with that holly bush. They shan't escape now."

Noddy placed the holly bush in front of the tree.

"Goblins, you are going to prison!" he shouted.

"Ow!" cried the goblins. "Ooh, ow!"

They couldn't escape!

Later on, Noddy told Mr Plod about his adventure.

"Well done, Noddy," said Mr Plod. "You deserve a reward. What would you like?"

"I should really like to carry on helping Big-Ears until you are better, Mr Plod," said Noddy. "But there's one more thing I would like. Could I have a proper police helmet?"

"You can try my spare helmet on," laughed Mr Plod.

"Thank you," said Noddy, putting the helmet on. "I shall look so important."

Poor Noddy! He didn't look important at all. In fact, he looked very, very funny!

You can now enjoy all your favourite
characters in Toybox books, audio and video tapes
and every month in Toybox Magazine